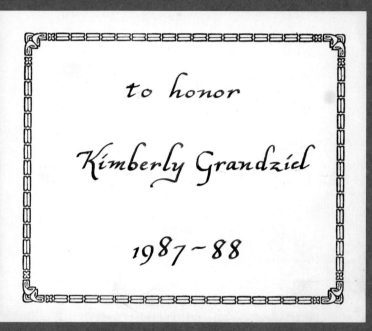

to honor

Kimberly Grandziel

1987 ~ 88

Hurry, Hurry, Mary Dear!

Hurry, Hurry, Mary Dear!

And Other Nonsense Poems

WRITTEN AND ILLUSTRATED
WITH PEN SKETCHES BY

N. M. Bodecker

MARGARET K. MCELDERRY BOOKS

New York

Margaret K. McElderry Books
Macmillan Publishing Company
866 Third Avenue
New York, NY 10022
Collier Macmillan Canada, Inc.

Manufactured in the United States of America by
Fairfield Graphics
Fairfield, Pennsylvania

First Edition

3   5   7   9   11   13   15   17   19——20   18   16   14   12   10   8   6   4

Library of Congress Cataloging-in-Publication Data

Bodecker, N. M.
    Hurry, hurry, Mary dear! and other nonsense poems.
    Reprint. Originally published: 1st ed. New York:
Atheneum, 1976.
    Summary: More of the Danish author's nonsense rhymes
complete with his own drawings.
    1. Nonsense-verses, American.   2. Children's poetry,
American.   [1. Nonsense verses]   I. Title.
[PS3552O33H8   1986]   811'.54   86-20998
ISBN 0-689-50066-1

880133

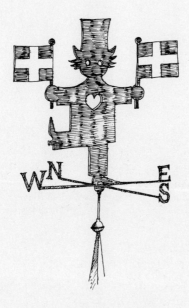

To Karlene Embler

Contents

HURRY, HURRY, MARY DEAR!

Hurry, hurry, Mary dear,
fall is over, winter's here.

Not a moment to be lost,
in a minute we get frost!

In an hour we get snow!
Drifts like houses! Ten below!

1

Pick the apples, dill the pickles,

chop down trees for wooden nickels.

Dig the turnips,

split the peas,

cook molasses,

curdle cheese.

Churn the butter,

smoke the hams,

can tomatoes,

put up jams.

Stack the stove wood, string the beans,

up the storms and down the screens.

Pull the curtains,

close the shutters.
Dreadfully the wild wind mutters.

Oil the snowshoes,

stoke the fires.
Soon the roads are hopeless mires.

Mend the mittens, knit the sweaters,
bring my glasses, mail my letters.

Toast the muffins, brew the tea,
hot and sweet and good for me.
Bake me doughnuts, plain and frosted . . .

What, my dear? You feel exhausted?

Yes, these winters are severe!
Hurry, hurry—

Mary dear.

BICKERING

The folks in Little Bickering
they argue quite a lot.
Is tutoring in bickering
required for a tot?
Are figs the best for figuring?
Is pepper ice cream hot?
Are wicks the best for wickering
a wicker chair or cot?
They find this endless dickering
and nonsense and nit-pickering
uncommonly invigor'ing,
I find it downright sickering!
You do agree!
Why not?

LONG JOHNS

First
they were too big,
then
they were too small.
I don't seem to remember
they ever fit at all.

I AM A CONSTANT WALKER

I am a constant walker,
I walk from place to place
with fierce determination
graven on my face.

I walk both late and early
(oh, it's an endless grind),
but never reach the places
that I set out to find.

I scramble to East Northfield
when aiming for West Rye,
I cannot walk like others
no matter how I try.

I trip in loops and doodles
across the straightest floors,
I trot for endless hours
trapped in revolving doors.

I walk in restless circles
at night, in moonlit squares;
I trudge disconsolately
up endless, spiral stairs.

But someone I met somewhere
took pains to make this point:
"Old man, that nose you follow
is crazy out of joint!"

And people say (in whispers)
when they deplore my fate:

"With a nose so like a corkscrew,
how could that guy go straight?"

A FOUNTAIN PEN POEM
(for S. C.)

This poem came out
of an old fountain pen
with this curious picture
of a little old hen
who had asked for spaghetti
but forgot to say: "When!"
(It's not what I hoped for,
I can tell you, but then
it's what *will* come out
of an old fountain pen.)

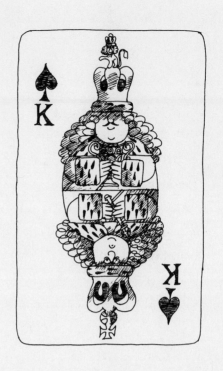

THE KING WHOSE CROWN
WAS UPSIDE DOWN

The King whose crown
was upside down
regarded with a surly frown
the King whose mop
and silver cup
and royal crown
were right side up.

But crowns and Kings
are changey things,
(one never knows
what fortune brings):
Kings have been found
to be de-crowned
when things (and Kings)
were turned around.

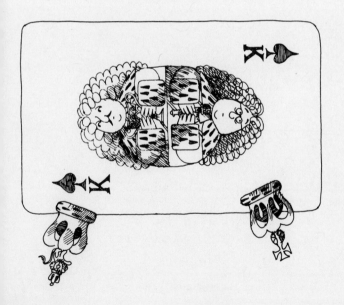

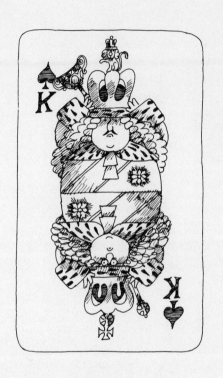

And that is why
with crafty eye
(may down be up
or ground be sky)
in ermine gowns
with surly frowns
they both cling tightly
to their crowns.

HOUSE FLIES

What makes
common house flies
trying
is
that they keep
multiflieing.

DEAR SYBIL

Dear Sybil,
   Is it proper
to wear a tall green hat,
when I go out to visit
my great-aunt Mrs. Pratt?

And should I wear a necktie
with one big, purple dot,
when having tea with someone
whose name, I think, is Pott?

And should my coat be wrinkled?
and should my shoes be creased?
and if my hat be sprinkled
with snuff, will she be pleased?

I'm happy to advise you:
when dining in a barn
your shoes as well as trousers
should be of crimson yarn.

A lettuce leaf is proper
suspended from the ear.
To wear Italian dressing
is very much too dear.

*A simple twist of lemon
or kumquat in the shoe,
does wonders for complexions
that are no longer new.*

Above all else remember:
It's always safe to come
in unobtrusive garments,
(though fashions vary some).

For every test conducted
has made it clear as ink:
TO DRESS AS I ADVISE YOU
BRINGS HAPPINESS!
I think.

A LITTLE BIT OF THIS, SIR

A little bit of this, Sir,
a little bit of that,
and you will be all right, Sir,
—unless you lose your hat.

But should you lose your hat, Sir,
(remember what it cost?)
you'll surely understand, Sir,
that everything is lost.

You could lose a little battle,
or perchance your little head,
but without that gorgeous hat, Sir,
you might as well be dead.

I'M SAD TODAY

I'm sad today.
I don't know why,
but sad enough
to want to cry,

and old enough
to make a song
of things today
that turned out wrong,

and wise enough,
as you can see,
to make this small song
cry for me.

POUNDCAKE FROM EALING

Poundcake from Ealing
and tea from Darjeeling
keep young pigs from squealing,
while tea
from other locations
restores the sensations
in wilted carnations
—when taken with jam from Dundee.

OCCUPATIONS

I've had many a strange occupation
and done many a curious thing,
since I came from a small, friendly nation
wrapped up in brown paper and string:

I have served as a crocodile tailor
(a maker of crocodiles' tails).

I have held a position as sailor,
(the person who holds up the sails),

I have waved where the oceans were waving,
and dined on monsoons and brown bread;
but I've never, no Jonathan, never
been a king with a crown on my head.

I once was a bee in a bonnet,

and half a brown bear in a play,

and a poet who wrote a sad sonnet
—but happily threw it away.

I have stood on my head on a steeple,
making speeches to folks who cried: "What?"
I've been asked to desist by most people
and have answered them: "Certainly not!"

I have stuck to my basic position,
when glued to a flexible sled;
but I've never, no Jonathan, never
been a king with a crown on my head.

I have lived among brooms in a closet
and been constantly swept off my feet.

I have grown an odd nose like a faucet
(a trick I shall never repeat).

I have had a most passionate yearning
to soar like a bird out of bounds,
but have turned as the breezes were turning,
—just a weather-dane doing his rounds.

I've been busy, but not very clever,
running races in slippers of lead;
so I've never, no Jonathan, never
been a king with a crown on my head.

But if they should come and inquire
if I would consent to be king,
I'd confess to a certain desire,
—that's not an unusual thing.

I'd say: "I was quite a good hummer,
once Mama had taught me to hum,
and I dare say I could be a plumber,
if someone would teach me to plumb.
And I'm certain I'd be just as merry
a king, dressed in ermine and red,
as any old Tom, Dick or Harry
with the crown of a king on his head."

THE RAIN IN MAINE

All day long it rained and rained,
and rained and rained in Maine.
And all day long we sat and sat
and looked out on the rain,

and thought: The sun will never come
and drive away the rain
that rains and rains and rains again
in Kennebunk in Maine.

But just before the day was done
the soggy clouds ran dry,
and the sun came out and winked at us
—with a raindrop in her eye.

MIDWINTER

As far as the eye can see,
nothing but woods and snow,
trees sticking up above
and roots, I suppose, below.

If you turned the world upside down,
the trees would be down below,
and as far as the eye could see
there'd be nothing but roots and snow.

FOR NEATNESS AND COMFORT

"For neatness and comfort,"
my grandfather said,
"Take off your boots
when you stand on your head."

"But," said Aunt Jane,
"does the boy understand
he should get a receipt
when he lends them a hand?"

"And have you implored him,"
inquired Aunt Sue,
"not to use toenails
where thumbtacks would do?"

"I have simply advised him,"
my grandfather said,
"to hold on to his hat
when he's losing his head."

OWNING UP

The wood duck didn't do it,
the woodcock didn't do it,
a dodo never did a thing like that!
And if whoever did it
is too finky to admit it
—whatever else he is, he's just a rat!

NEVER MIND THE RAIN

Never mind the rain!
It doesn't leave a stain.

Never mind the snow!
It melts before you know.

But rain and snow together!
That's pretty nasty weather.

MILTON TRIMMER

Milton Trimmer, ardent swimmer,
swam to slim but got no slimmer;
on the contrary, he grew
(most alarming thing to view)
like a huge, inflated beach ball
where the offshore breezes blew.

And they cautioned him: "Oh, Trimmer,
rapidly ballooning swimmer,
where the whales and breakers roar
kindly swim about no more,
but rejoin us, we implore you,
on the safe and solid shore."

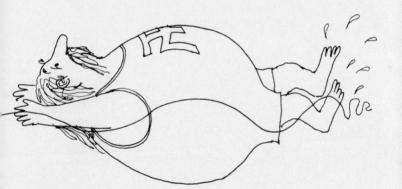

When he swam above a breaker,
people said: "He's just a faker."

When he swam above the sea,
people said: "How can it be?"

When he swam above the mountain,
people said: "It's most astoundin',
but he does appear to float
on the breezes like a boat,
and he hasn't got a license,
and he hasn't got a crew,
and he's bound to cross horizons
though his suit is hardly new.

And they wrung their hands in sorrow,
and they wept in their despair,
and they cried: "Perhaps tomorrow
he will be—we know not where!"

When he swam into the distance,
and the moon was thin and new,
people said: "He must have pistons,
or propellers, or a screw.
Note the way he turns his ankle,
could his engine be a Wankel?
or some secret new propellant
that's imbedded in his toe?
We confess we do not know.

When the darkness hid the mountain
and the breakers and the shore,

they went home and never, ever
mentioned Trimmer any more.

INK HATS

In a dreary place
I know,
silent clumps
of ink hats grow.

Full of poems,
one should think,
since their hats
are full of ink.

But they vanish
in their place,
leaving not a blot or trace,

that a human eye
can see,
of their inky
poetry.

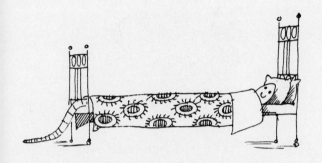

NIGHT CRAWLER

Night crawler,
night crawler,
poor little creep,
don't crawl about now
but go home and sleep.
Crawl into bed now
and don't stay up late.
Late night crawlers
end up as bait.

THE HAT, THE GOWN
AND THE RING

My mother she wore
a beautiful hat,
a sunflower pot,
something like that.
She sometimes said "yes"
and sometimes said "no,"
depending on what
made her sunflowers grow.

My mother she wore
a beautiful gown
of newspaper clippings
from all over town.
She sometimes said "no"
and sometimes said "yes,"
depending on what
she would read on her dress.

My mother she wore
a beautiful ring
from a nursery curtain
they cleaned in the spring.
Some thought she looked silly,
I thought she looked dear
with her hat and her gown
and that ring in her ear.

WHEN ALL THE WORLD
IS FULL OF SNOW

I never know
just where to go,
when all the world
is full of snow.

I do not want
to make a track,
not even
to the shed and back.

I only want
to watch and wait,
while snow moths settle
on the gate,

and swarming frost flakes
fill the trees
with billions
of albino bees.

I want to watch
the snow swarms thin,
'til all my bees
have settled in,

and on the ice
the boulders ride,
like sleeping snow geese
on the tide.

I only want
myself to be
as silent as
a winter tree,

to hear the swirling
stillness grow,
when all the world
is full of snow.

THE DOVES STAY IN THEIR COTES

The doves stay in their cotes,
the hens stay in their sheds,

the ducklings in the duck pond
keep standing on their heads.

The little boys and girls
refuse to leave their beds,

for it's raining cats and dogs
—and other quadrupeds.

SING ME A SONG OF
TEAPOTS AND TRUMPETS

Sing me a song
of teapots and trumpets:
Trumpots and teapets
And tippets and taps,
trippers and trappers
and jelly bean wrappers
and pigs in pajamas
with zippers and snaps.

Sing me a song
of sneakers and snoopers:
Snookers and sneapers
and snappers and snacks,
snorkels and snarkles,
a seagull that gargles,
and gargoyles and gryphons
and other knickknacks.

Sing me a song
of parsnips and pickles:
Picsnips and parkles
and pumpkins and pears,
plumbers and mummers
and kettle drum drummers
and plum jam (yum-yum jam)
all over their chairs.

Sing me a song—
but never you mind it!
I've had enough
of this nonsense. Don't cry.
Criers and fliers
and onion ring fryers—
It's more than I want to put up with!
Good-by!

GETTING READY

Wash your hands neatly
with Number 1 dirt,
add water as needed,
then put on your shirt.

Shampoo your hair
with molasses and brine
(add oatmeal for body
and honey for shine).

Add gum drops for flavor
and fish glue for "stick."
You'll certainly love it
—unless you get sick.

Rinse in sweet cider
(or tea if you choose).
Yummy the way
it runs into your shoes.

Then stick on your bow tie
with marshmallow jam
and cry to your mother:
"It's ready I am!"

Say to her (sweetly):
"I'm ready to go—"
and hear that dear peace-loving
person go: "O-o-o-o-h! NO!"

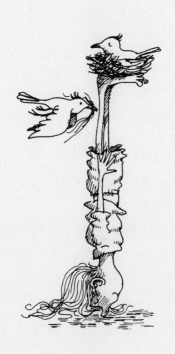

WHEN YOU STAND
ON THE TIP OF YOUR NOSE

When you stand on the tip of your nose,
keeping perfectly still,
while the birds build their nests twixt
    your toes,
as they certainly will,
speak kind and encouraging words,
don't wiggle however it goes,
as you might inconvenience the birds
or scramble their eggs with your toes.

81

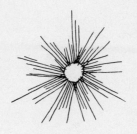

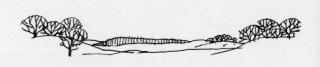

DAY MOON

Some days, when the sun is high,
the moon is also in the sky.
Why is it then that, warm and bright,
the sun does never shine at night?

MORNING FOG

Fog in all the hedges,
good for frog and toad,
fog in drifts and patches
along the morning road.

Fog in fields and hollows,
curling in the glades,
hiding autumn grasses,
pearling on their blades,

clothing rocks and hillocks
in its ghostly gray.
In case you had forgotten:
today is ground-fog-day.

GARDEN CALENDAR

When the dogstar is aglow
plant petunias in the snow.

When the snow begins to melt
wrap your hollyhocks in felt.

When the felt begins to bloom
pick the apples off your broom.

When the broom begins to wear
weed the turnips in your chair.

When the chair begins to rock
prune the snowdrops in your sock.

When the sock is full of holes
blame the whole thing on the moles.

When the moles inquire: "Why pick on us?" Say simply, "I

will instruct you how to grow pink petunias in the snow."

THE LADY IN YELLOW

The lady in yellow
was sunny and mellow
and rode on an ox
with a very nice fellow.
She played the French horn,
he played the cello
but hit a bum note
that made the ox bellow
—at which she dismissed
that a-musical fellow.

ONE YEAR

January played
a cold tin flute.

February sat
by the fire with a lute.

March was a penny whistle
sharp, cheap, clear.

April was a drummer
with a green bandolier.

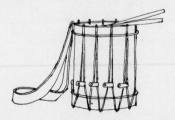

May was a bird call
in the brave new wood.

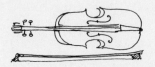

June was a violin
that played as it should.

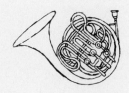

July was a French horn,
a hunt going past.

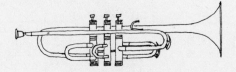

August was a hot-lipped
jazz-trumpet blast.

September was a zither
with a fine mellow string.

October was the woodwinds
waiting in the wing.

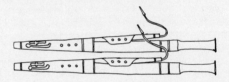

November was an oboe,
plaintive and glum.

December was the boom
of the deep kettle drum.

MY FATHER HE WAS
A CRANKY OLD MAN

My father he was
a cranky old man,
he walked in the woods
where the dark river ran.
He whittled two flutes
from the bog willow tree:
one was for my sister
and one was for me,
but whenever we asked him
to teach us to play,
"Whittledownderry"
was all he would say.
"Whittledown
wattledown
derry-dory-down,
waydown
waterdown
willow."

He whittled two flutes
with his pearl-handled knife,
but played only one tune
all his long life:
The Song of the Rain
in the Bog Willow Tree.
He played it for my sister
and he played it for me,
but whenever we asked him
to please tell us why,
"Wattledown worry"
was all his reply.
"Whittledown
wattledown
hurry-worry-down
waydown
waterdown
willow."

THE LADY IN GOLD

The lady in gold
was terribly old,
and crusty and cranky
and lonely and cold.
She lived in a mansion,
all mildew and mold,
alone with the wind
in her dress made of old,
durable gold.

PENNY SONG

Penny pincher,
penny. pincher,
what are you to me?
If you want a silver dollar
there's a full moon in the tree.
I can give you notes aplenty,
of willow thrush and finch,
but I haven't got a penny
for anyone to pinch.
I haven't got a nickel,
I haven't got a dime,
and I wouldn't give a penny
for your penny-pinching time!

Penny feather,
penny feather,
what are we to do?
The evening all around us
is periwinkle blue.
There are mists in fields and hedges
and crickets singing there,
and I'm beneath the moon tree
with a feather in my hair,
and I wonder, and I wonder—
oh, an endlessness of things—
while the sky is growing purple
with penny-feather wings.

Penny whistle,
penny whistle,
what is there to play?
The beaches and the oceans
are white and silver gray:
wide and white and empty,
like deserts in the moon—
emptiness and silence—
a penny for a tune!
A penny for a whistle
to tell me where to go,
a penny for tomorrow.
Blow, penny whistle, blow!

THE LADY IN WHITE

The lady in white
was a spirit or sprite,
who kept people in castles
awake in the night.
She wore a lace gown,
all wispy and light,
that glowed as she groaned,
in the dead of the night,
just out of spite.

MY DAD HE WAS A YANKEE

My dad he was a Yankee,
my granddad was a Dane,
my great-granddad was an Irishman,
born in the heart of Spain.

MICE ARE NICE

Mice
are nice,
and sprigs
of spice,
and jelly beans
and jingles.
Kids
are nice,
but twins
are twice
as nice, they say,
as singles.

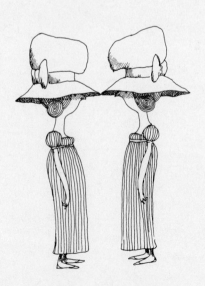

GOOD-BY MY WINTER SUIT

Good-by my winter suit,
good-by my hat and boot,
good-by my ear-protecting muffs
and storms that hail and hoot.

Farewell to snow and sleet,
farewell to Cream of Wheat,
farewell to ice-removing salt
and slush around my feet.

Right on! to daffodils,
right on! to whippoorwills,
right on! to chirp-producing eggs
and baby birds and quills.

The day is on the wing,
the kite is on the string,
the sun is where the sun should be—
it's spring all right! It's spring!

NEVER, EVER
LET THEM KNOW

Never, ever
let them know
where the wild
strawberries grow.

Never, ever
tell them when
they are sweet
and ripe again.

Never? Ever?
Then it's true—
someone grew them
just for you?

SUNFLOWERS

One frosty evening
the sunflowers set,
their great necks broken.
Pile and forget.

Under the rakings
of leaves and weeds
new suns are sleeping
in buried seeds.

They will awaken
and greet your eyes
midsummer mornings
at sunflower rise.

THIS IS ELMER JOHNSON
(*for E. B.*)

This is Elmer Johnson,
he's a parakeet,
posing in his jumpsuit.
Isn't Elmer neat?

Braver than an eagle,
brighter than a coot,
jumping from the treetops
in his parachute.

Goggles on his nose tip,
muffler round his chin,
steering with his tail
—and a little para'fin.

Dangling like a gumdrop,
isn't Elmer sweet,
little parasols
on his little parafeet,

Tugging at his chute strings,
heart strings too, you bet,
and landing in the clover
—the little parapet.

WHEN KINGS WORE CROWNS

When kings wore crowns for breakfast
the world was rather new,
and people never minded
the odd things kings would do.

But now the world is older,
kings have grown rather rare
and somewhat more particular
about the things they wear.

They don't want to be different,
or leastways not in looks,
but dress like other common folk
in suits and hats from Brooks.

Crowns are severely frowned upon
as not at all the thing.
Good night, most splendid Majesty.
Good morning, Mr. King.

UNDER MY HAT IS MY HAIR

Under my hat is my hair,
under my hair is my head,
under my head is a seven-yard beard
and a tie that is yellow and red.

Under my tie is my coat,
under my coat is my vest,
under my vest is a thing that goes bump!
like a chicken heart inside my chest.

Inside that thing is a grin,
like a Cheshire cat's, stuck in a tree.
Take away the odd tie and the rest,
and the grin that is left—that's me.

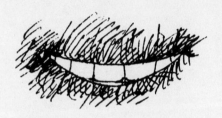